MW01091925

For my mom, Elizabeth, and the grandbabies she loved most in all the world. Your love is still felt every day.

And for anyone who has lost someone incredibly dear to them — their love is with you always.

Justine Jackson
Camas, Washington

justinewritesbooks.com

Names: Jackson, Justine, author. | Nielsen, Megan, illustrator.
Title: Grammy Lamby / Justine Jackson ; illustrated by Megan Nielsen.
Description: Camas, WA : Justine Jackson, 2023. | Summary: Walk alongside LiPle Lamby as he comes to terms with the loss of his beloved Grammy Lamby. |
Audience: Grades K-3.
Identifiers: LCCN 2022917935 (print) | ISBN 979-8-9868397-0-7 (hardcover) |
ISBN 979-8-9868397-1-4 (paperback)
Subjects: LCSH: Picture books for children. | CYAC: Grandparent and child--Fiction. | Grief--Fiction. | Loss--Fiction. | Immortality--Fiction. | BISAC: JUVENILE FICTION / Social Themes / Death, Grief, Bereavement. | JUVENILE FICTION / Family / General.
Classification: LCC PZ7.1.J33 Gr 2023 (print) | LCC PZ7.1.J33 (ebook) | DDC [E]--dc23.

Book Design by Arlene Soto, Intricate Designs
Photo of Justine by Chris Jackson

GRAMMY
Lamby

By Justine Jackson
Illustrated by Megan Nielsen

Today is the day!
It's finally here!

"Grammy Lamby is coming!"
I excitedly cheer.

I get up and stretch,

A big grin on my face.

Then I leap down the hall
At the speediest pace.

I dash to my mama,
And start to explain,
Plans for Grammy and me,
But her eyes fill with pain.

She pulls me in close,
I sense the dismay,
She takes a deep breath
And then starts to say...

Grammy Lamby can't come play,
Grammy Lamby's gone away.
But Grammy Lamby's always near,
Even when she's not right here.

You may wonder, "Where did she go?"

We all have ideas,
But only those
we've lost know.

But Grammy Lamby's in your heart
Her love for you will never part.
She lives on through the love she left.
Her time with you was her greatest gift.

Grammy Lamby can *still* be found

Her memory is all around.

From the gifts she gave to the giggles you shared,
Grammy's love is still everywhere!

When missing her feels too much to bear,
Know that feeling sad shows the love
you shared. Grammy Lamby feels this too,
And would give anything to be with you.

So, on those days it's feeling tough,
Know that no time would ever be enough.
Take a deep breath and remember the love,
And know Grammy's proud and watching
over from above.

4 x 6

Your loved one's spirit is like an ember,
It glows brightly when you remember.
What are some of your favorite memories together?

Tell them to your loved one HERE.

About the Author

Justine Jackson is an elementary school teacher whose personal experiences with grief and passion for children's books propelled her into writing one of her very own— a book she once longed to have for her own children after the loss of her dear mother. Justine Jackson is a creative at heart and resides in the Pacific Northwest.

Find her online at
justinewritesbooks.com   @justinewritesbooks

About the Illustrator

Megan Nielsen is the owner and illustrator of Little Pine Artistry. There she offers many different products of her artwork. This is Megan's first illustrated book. Originally from Seattle, Washington she now lives with her family and two dogs in Central Oregon. Megan connected with Justine over their shared loss of their mothers too early.

Find her online at
littlepineartistry.com   @littlepineartistry